W9-CNA-816

The Three Billy Goats Gruff

Retold by **Mary Finch**
Illustrated by **Roberta Arenson**

Barefoot Books
Celebrating Art and Story

Once upon a time there were three billy goats gruff. There was a little billy goat gruff, a middle-sized billy goat gruff and a big billy goat gruff.

The three billy goats gruff lived in a field and they spent their days munching the green grass. On one side of the field there was a stream, and over the stream there was a rickety bridge.

On the other side of the rickety bridge there was a hill, and there the grass grew greener and sweeter than it did in the field of the billy goats gruff.

Under the rickety bridge lived a big,
hairy troll in a deep dark hole.

It was damp and cold under the bridge and that made the troll furious. He was also hungry.

One day the little billy goat gruff looked up and saw that the grass up the hill on the other side of the stream looked very green and sweet.

"I think I'll move over there for my next course," he said. "Then I'll grow big and fat."

So, trip, trap, trip, trap, went the hooves of the little billy goat gruff as he started to cross the rickety bridge.

The big, hairy troll woke up with a start.

"Who's that crossing my bridge?" he roared.

"I am," said the little billy goat gruff.

"I'm crossing the bridge to eat the grass on the other side of the stream."

"Oh no, you're not," said the big, hairy troll. And he sang,

> "I'm a troll, from a deep dark hole,
> My belly's getting thinner,
> I need to eat — and goat's a treat —
> So I'll have you for my dinner."

"Oh, don't do that," said the little billy goat gruff. "I'm only small — I wouldn't make much of a mouthful. Wait for my brother — he's much bigger." And he skipped over the rickety bridge to the other side.

Just then the middle-sized billy goat gruff looked
up and he, too, saw that the grass on the other
side of the stream looked very green and sweet.

"I think I'll move over there for my next course,"
he said. "Then I'll grow bigger and fatter."

So, trip, trap, trip, trap, went the hooves of the middle-sized billy goat gruff as he started to cross the rickety bridge.

"Who's that crossing my bridge?" roared the big, hairy troll.

"I am," said the middle-sized billy goat gruff. "I'm crossing the bridge to eat the grass on the other side of the stream."

"Oh no, you're not," said the big, hairy troll. And he sang,

"I'm a troll, from a deep dark hole,
My belly's getting thinner.
I need to eat — and goat's a treat —
So I'll have you for my dinner."

"Oh, don't do that," said the middle-sized billy goat gruff. "I'm not very big — I wouldn't make much of a mouthful. Wait for my brother — he's much, much bigger." And he skipped over the rickety bridge to the other side.

Just then the big billy goat gruff looked up and he, too, saw that the grass on the other side of the stream looked very green and sweet.

"I think I'll move over there for my next course," he said. "Then I'll grow even bigger and fatter."

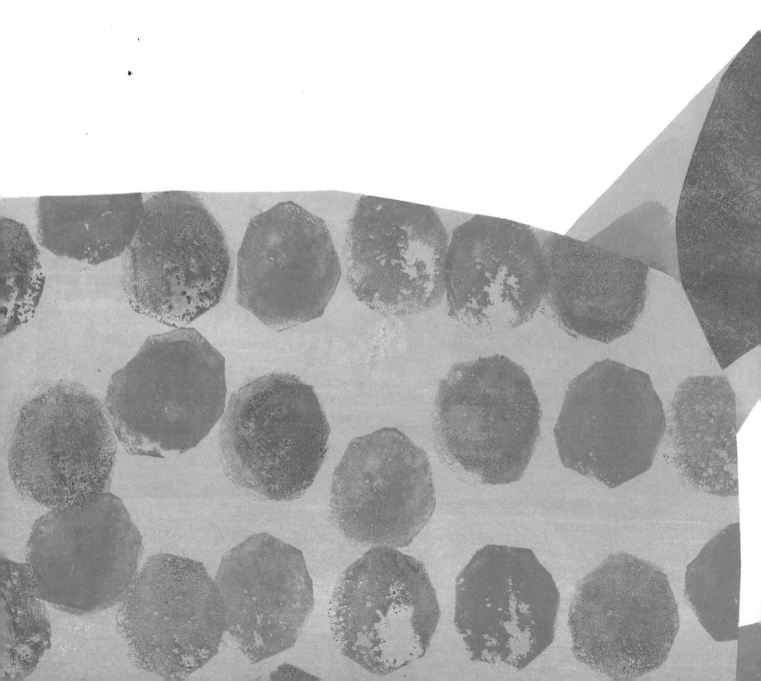

So trip, trap, trip, trap, went the hooves of the big billy goat gruff as he started to cross the rickety bridge.

"Who's that crossing my bridge?" roared the big, hairy troll.

"I am," said the big billy goat gruff. "I'm crossing the bridge to eat the grass on the other side of the stream."

"Oh no, you're not," said the big, hairy troll. And he sang,

"I'm a troll, from a deep dark hole,
My belly's getting thinner,
I need to eat — and goat's a treat —
So I'll have you for my dinner."

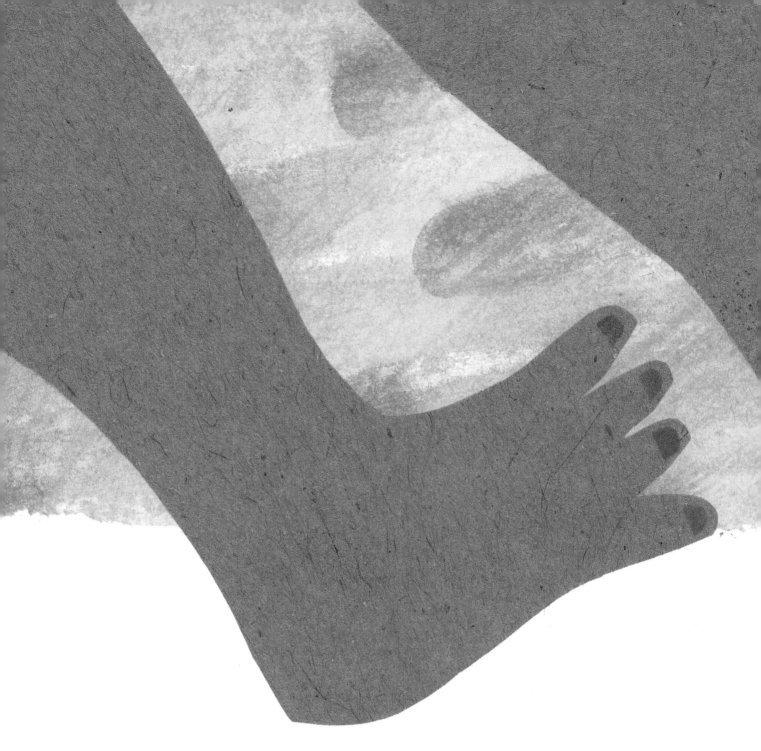

The big billy goat gruff stopped. His knees shook, his hooves trembled, clickety clack, clickety clack, on the rickety bridge. Then he pulled himself together. "I don't think you will," he said.

And he picked up his hooves and kicked the troll into the middle of next week!

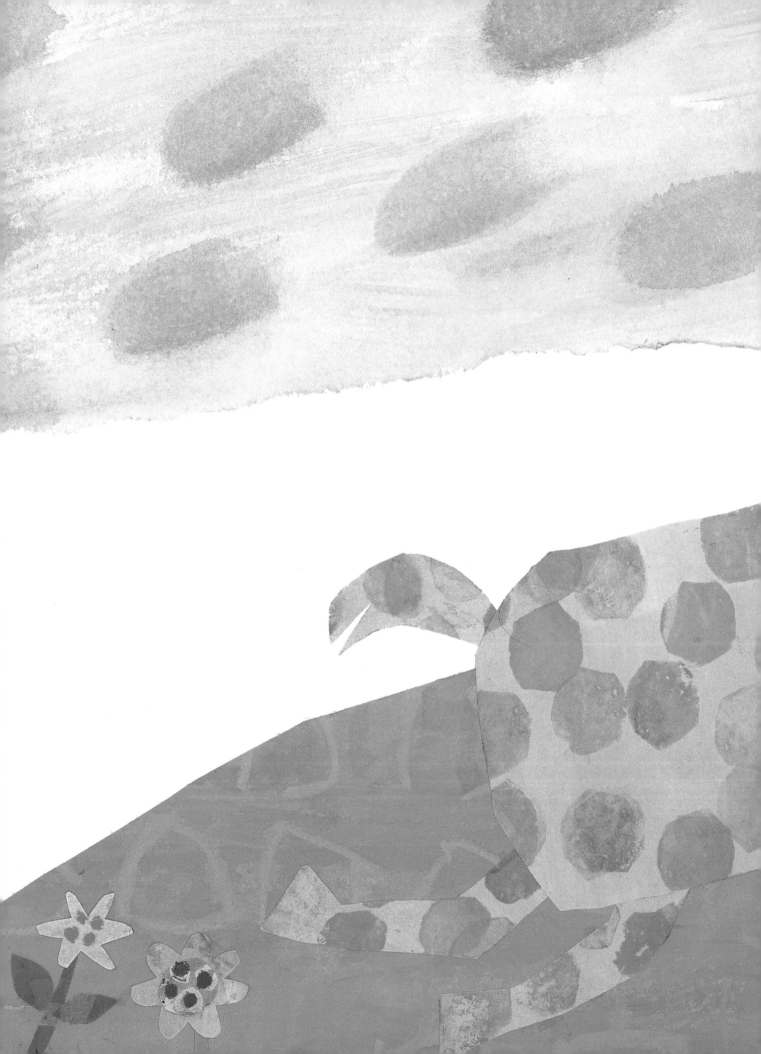

Then the big billy goat gruff skipped over
the rickety bridge to join his brothers
on the other side of the hill.

As for the big, hairy troll, I am happy to say that he was never seen again.